Prelude:

Audrey was up in San Francisco. The same
city I had fled to a year prior. It had been a
sad and saintly arrival to San Francisco; a
respite, for a sojourner who followed a trail
to Mecca but was left without hope when
faith itself had failed. I had read Kerouac
and gotten the wrong idea. A life on the road
wasn't for me. I wanted the cities and all
their promise. Mostly I wanted to get her
back. I had pulled into a motel off
University Ave., in Berkeley. My days were
marked by the constant drone of reality
T.V., and beers sat empty in the dismal
clutter of the motel room.

It was these days that I wondered to myself
if this city was saintly in name only. Or was
its saintliness only reserved for the devout,
not the lost boys of the West? Not those who
sought salvation in times when running was
mistaken for a sense of pilgrimage? This had
been no way to live; just as it was no way to
live up in the hills in Mendocino; smoking
blunts in an empty state; looking after the
neighbor's daughter; watching old reruns of
cartoons on T.V., trimming weed and
drinking to pass the time. There had been
better days than this, but not for a long
while. The money ran out, and I moved to

the Mission, to Audrey's apartment, who didn't ask questions but laid out a cot on her living room floor. She didn't mind I showed up unexpected; she didn't mind a lot of things.

My life had turned into strange sorry Americana, like it had been moving from town to town, living with fervor, escaping depression. Now, I burned down heaters and drank steadily. I warded off the despair I felt, but would never admit to. This was not unknown to Audrey. She took it upon herself at Mission Park one afternoon.

"Frank," she said, "What's happened?"

I knew my run up the West Coast was over and cried. Audrey and I held each other, hardly clasping one another on a shoreline outside of the City. San Francisco itself sat across the bay like a half-remembered dream. I composed myself like a woman does and packed up my things and left that same night. For days, I wandered San Francisco. The Mission's streets seemed empty, but I moved about the bustle of people, glancing at strangers, hoping someone would look at me with mercy. Where I found none, I questioned if I was capable of loving someone else. Audrey wasn't the one, but she had tried. And for that, I was heartbroken. Sad solemn poetry ran through my head like Buddhist mantras of the East.

It had been our dream.

1

I was tearing down a bungalow in Beverly Hills with the handsome prince Dean Jones. Dean would remark that "it is a sentimental thing tearing down a home." I remarked that it was strange that we could feel anything at all about something so arbitrary as ripping out drywall. But, I was having my own fraught experience staring down the guts of this bungalow in Beverly Hills; wondering what my life would look like if the last of it was torn down. Would anything be left at all?

I shared a room with Damian. Damian was a good Catholic kid with a sweet demeanor, who had been graced with a pen he couldn't put down. Life for Damian was filled with zest and gusto. He was 6'0 tall with strawberry blonde hair. He walked around shirtless and there wasn't an ounce of fat on his wiry frame. He wore a navy-blue bucket hat and socks with sandals. He was pseudo spiritual. Still, his mantras persisted.

Each morning after he meditated on the balcony that overlooked the drive, I would have a smoke. Damian kept a close eye on me, especially the days I was parked in front of the television, consuming information about America's War on Terror. I told him not to worry, "it's just a phase." Audrey must have been worried, because she texted me, "Frank, Damian said you're on another military kick." "That's right," I replied. "You promised me you wouldn't join the military if you moved to L.A." Audrey replied. "I'm not going to, they wouldn't let me join, something about mental instability," I wrote back.

2

Dean asked me about the Marines. Dean wasn't the judgmental type, but he was the discerning kind. There was some determination to believe my interest in the army wasn't some delusion that had been cooked up in the desert. It wasn't a boyish fantasy. But it was the only way Frank Bernard could beat a case. Frank Bernard wasn't patriotic, but he was loyal to his country. Just like the boys who took a knee and the boys who returned from our forgotten wars in the Middle East.

God damn them for thinking otherwise.

The Los Angeles air gave me headaches. Smoking too many cigarettes gave me a cough. Damian suggested I drink more water, go vegan and take up his meditation practice. Damian was the romantic I always purported to be. I was the hopeless romantic I never wanted to become.

It was a relationship born out of necessity.

It had been a humid affair that summer in Boston when we became friends. Hot air seeped through air conditioners and the stale smell of cigarettes congested vents.
It was always with Damian that my mind would bend back to the dharma. He spoke about it like he knew something. I acted like I didn't.

Karma is what bound us together, and the same went for sin. The church was in neck deep with the Temple.

Curse them all.

Damian and I would find refuge in the shade of the courtyards that filled the museums, writing crap poetry about the girls that had once had our hearts. We played basketball in the fens. Damian won every game, but he always gave me a shot. We drank cold coffees and bargained with the unrelenting summer heat. Damian had rented film equipment from the college, and he would chase me around Boston making short films that would never see the light of day.

I worked at a French cafe in Fenway, whose patrons were mostly internationals. I would overhear French conversations in the corner in the cafe and my heart would race. My eyes sometimes became wet but I never cried. And I didn't run from these moments. Damian and his roommate Annie B. would visit the cafe and distract me from my sadness. So did Sasha and veiled women that moved like ghosts through the silent nights.

I lived across the street from the cafe and they lived across from the park. Damian, Annie B. and I spent our nights faded at the dive bar on the corner, smoking cigarettes on my stoop and planning the rest of our lives.

There were a few girls before I met her. The girls before were Maria and Ciara, and a handful not worth mentioning. But it was Josie's absence that left me short of breath in the humid air that stuck to my lungs like glue. The right word was gutted. There had been her, and then she had been gone. And I am not too stubborn as to admit I cried the morning she left Boston for Paris: leaving me with the remnants of a romance shared when winter had been the coldest.

Michele was my only outlet.

We lived in a hole in the wall on Peterborough, in an aging apartment that's smallness forced us together. Some days he needed a break from my stories, some days he listened and offered advice. "I saw her walking down Newbury," he told me days before she left. "You're going to marry that girl."

She had been gone before Spring had turned into a humid summer. Beautiful winter is what she had called it; when the snow and sleet pounded Boston in big unrelenting gusts of wind that shot across the city from the Boston Harbor to the Charles River.

Depression had plagued me through my collegiate years:

1) The times when I would sit in my room smoking blunts in a placid state during frozen winter, struggling to find the right words to begin my half-plagiarized term papers that evaded my professor's eyes.

2) The times when I would consume myself

in dharma talks at the local ashram hoping to regain some sort of nostalgia for my depression-less days biking around Asia searching for a God that could cure my fractured psyche that had been so broken in the West.

3) The times when I would take a bus down to Chinatown just to think about her, believing I lost her when spring brought Boston back to life.

Damian told me he believed I enjoyed suffering. "Life is to be lived, amigo." His reminders were of no use to me but Damian did everything he could do to breathe life back into me when she was gone. We watched movies in his flat. We ate cheeseburgers and drank milkshakes from the diner down the street. We went for long walks along the Charles that snaked across the river into Cambridge

I had been alone my whole life seeking someone else who would make my beliefs feel real. She had.

But there was Damian and there was poetry.

3

Shady palm trees lined the streets in Los Angeles. They grew in groves in the corners where day workers would collect, drinking beers and smoking cigarettes. Palm leaves became discarded in the gutters and the palms themselves cast long shadows across the streets and made impressions on the mansions that were a stone's throw from the Koreatown tenements that crowded everything East of Larchmont.

I'd walk to work every day at dawn, waking up in my clothes, throwing on shoes and marching to the cafe on Larchmont Boulevard, sleep still sticking to my eyes.

The mornings would be cool, but warm enough to make a sweat.

"This walk would be harder in the military, so "enjoy it while you can." Of course, joining the military also meant giving up antidepressants. It was a double-edged sword.

It was the farthest cry from my once monastic like tendencies. But I wanted to do something that was greater than myself

when all I needed to do was count breaths,
like I did everyday 20 cigarettes deep,
writing out a rendition of On the Road that
Baldwin himself would have written-off.

Yet, it was in Los Angeles that I sought
myself in the margins of America, working
paycheck to paycheck, splitting the
apartment with Damian, cramming two twin
beds into the lone bedroom, working the
coffeehouse, tearing down the home with
Dean Jones.

It was a hardscrabble life I wouldn't
willingly give up.

It was also in Los Angeles that my mother
was convinced that her only son had become
a conspiracy theorist. Every god damn Uber
driver was in with the Feds. Every god damn
drive was an interrogation like I was a
radical Black nationalist. Every God damn
time an Uber driver asked if I believed in
God I played dumb.

 I told one driver about my inspiration:
 the Beat generation.

The next day a pile of red beets were at my
door step.

I cooked them for dinner.

The next Uber driver who asked me what I wanted to do in life got a load of bullshit.

"Drive a train across the country."

A year later I rode a train from Buffalo to Boston 10 deep off vodka sodas writing a story so sick that only an FBI agent would believe it.

Some life, huh?

In Los Angeles guys like Leo and Pacino had once been as unknown as me. They had made it through the ranks to become the bossmen in Hollywood.

In Los Angeles thousands of children with "Dreams," got scammed by pay to play theatre classes and auditions for commercial agents that were in it for a big buck.

What a waste.

At the playhouse, my peers got gassed up by acting teachers that never had a chance in hell to make it out of the Hollywood gutters. My battle with the Feds was just beginning and my battle with the bottle was ongoing.

But my dreams, they were still alive. In the end, it was not at all very liberating, just difficult, and nerve-wracking.

My only solace came at a café across from the Playhouse where they treated me like their son and let me run up my bill while I wasted money on Uber's to the Life Transformation Center for Mental Health & Vitality to please my mother.

"You will be OK Francis, you have a good heart."

Damian asked me if I wanted to give meditation a chance on some retreat up North. I would do anything to get out of L.A. I was fighting through the aches and pains. These were ten hours of labor, six days a week, hauling debris from the house into the dumpster that sat in the street. I got 45 minutes a day for lunch.

Dean and I would drive into Culver City to pick up something to eat. Dean had always found me curious. He would pepper me with questions about religion and spirituality. When I told Dean I believed in God, he told me he did not. He told me he believed in science, and that the general laws of physics explained our existence. God had some sort of great plan for me, but I never shared these plans with Dean because of his avowed atheism. Dean was also a model and actor. I was not. God's greatest plans were for non-believers.

Meditation was the only way out of town, so Damian rented a car and took off up North, up the 1, through Big Sur, stopping for gas and ice cream in Carmel. There, in the hills of Marin County, up past San Francisco, at an ashram where meditation began every day at sunrise; I slept through Tai Chi and after three days of "meditating" (which caused lower back pain and racing thoughts) I was ready to drive back to L.A., break sobriety and get loaded in a dive bar off the sunset strip.

I had a pack of cigarettes in the car, and would grab them and disappear once a day and walk deep into the hills that surrounded the meditation hall. I was convinced half the retreat was in with the F.B.I. But I kept it to myself, for Damian's sake, and my own.

Damian and I shared a room but Damian had taken a vow of silence. I had not. But I was too afraid to speak. The silence was consuming; I didn't know what words would leave my mouth; hearing my own thoughts;

believing I was going crazy; I walked in circles; shifting around on my cushion; I was the loudest person in the meditation hall; Everyone was busy hijacking their nervous system and reciting mantras except for me.

When it was my turn to meet the guru leading the retreat, he told me "You better have another plan," when I told him I had moved to L.A. to become an actor. I was paying for his honesty, not his kindness. Getting loaded on the sunset strip now seemed like the best option to find enlightenment.

By day seven I could see the light at the end of the tunnel. I stopped hearing my thoughts, and listened to my breath. Damian had begun to flaunt a half-smile on his face, he was enjoying himself.

I had been taken hostage and marooned on a remote island, forced to fend for myself. I slept through the morning meditation, all the way until breakfast. The food was vegetarian. I craved bacon, or sausage. Part of me started to believe Damian just brought me here to convert me into a vegan.

The second morning and the eighth day,

Damian shot me a wink at breakfast. He knew I was breaking. I was becoming softer, kinder and farther away from my delusions. Or perhaps, I was just sleeping more. I still escaped to the car and smoked cigarettes in the hills. My thoughts wandered. But they always led back to her. I wondered if I'd get her back. I wondered if I would ever see her again. It was terribly unfair. I wanted her gone, but she was here to stay.

The guru told me it was a confusing time to be a man in this country. "Hold yourself in loving awareness, these days are not easy," he said. Easy times, there hadn't been any since the night we met, and recited mantras and sat in lotus position. Sometimes I curled up into a child's pose. When it was all over, oh what a feeling. Damian and I embraced. "I know you could do it," he said.

We got back on the road to Los Angeles, and Damian suggested I give the audiobooks he bought at the meditation center a chance: "We all have a loyalty to our pain, to the stories we tell. We have some faith that clinging or holding onto them is going to work, and clinging is some way does work, it kind of works to bring some happiness, but the Buddha said clinging can't fulfil what the heart actually wants. Letting go can."

4

Where she had once been a part of my life, she had become a memory that had taken me to a town built on the dreams of a few, and the delusions of many. I was nostalgic for romance we never truly had. In Los Angeles I had a vision of celebrity that couldn't be unwritten in my head. But the spectacle of fame was running its course (depression still lingered).

"What will you do when you finish school?" She had asked me one night as she held onto my arm as we walked through campus. "Go West, and take you with me." I had replied.

We were supposed drive across beautiful America. It was supposed to be her and I. It wasn't supposed to be with Jacque, or Felix or a Loris or whatever French boyfriend she had. She was going to ditch him while we drove through Texas. She was going to take her top off as some sort of radical political statement. She was going to paint watercolors in her underwear in Topanga while I drank lemonade and she smoked sativa. Oh well. Maybe in another life.

"Everything is gonna be alright, buddy."
Damian said, after I told him I scrolled
through her social. He was on his way out
the door to his girlfriend Sasha's. Sasha was
rich. She lived in a sprawling apartment
complex in West Hollywood, a few blocks
off the boulevard. There was a pool in the
middle of the complex where we would go
swimming when the temperatures exceeded
100 Fahrenheit.

Damian was leaving me to my own devices.
I didn't see him for the rest of the month.
We cooked together, we ate together, we
wrote together, we read together, we drank
coffee together, we did everything except
sleep with each other.

Sasha took care of him. She looked out for
me, too. Thank god for small miracles.

I started taking kickboxing classes in a
gymnasium close to the subway station on
Western and Wilshire but I was never one
for athletics. I got in the ring and sparred
with men who knocked me into the ropes; I
swinging with deftness; but the fights were
always lopsided. A drug dealer called me
"Benny" and asked me if I wanted to go for
a ride.

I told him I didn't know him.

He told me:

"You know me but you don't want to know me."

I didn't want to know anybody.

I went for walks deeper and deeper into Koreatown. If my phone rang I let it go to voicemail. I would walk as far as East L.A., into the barrio and onto a bus home. Advertisements in Korean, then Spanish would sit in windows of bodegas and insurance companies.

This was America:

The immigrants, the poor, the overworked and non-unionized, the day laborers and the home health aides. This was where dreams were born, but never realized. This is where I thought mine would die.

I was lovesick and I did everything but drink (the only solution I ever had). I thought of her and touched myself in the shower. This was no relief, just a release. I became less determined to become famous and more determined to find some meaning in a life that was meant for her.

I would walk down Western and eat Korean BBQ alone. I listened to Elliot Smith. I watched bad movies with English subtitles. I stood outside the Marine recruiting office and thought about throwing away my anti-depressants. Instead, I took the tram across town to Santa Monica and sat through sermons at St. Monica's Catholic Church.

I left early and walked out near the promenades. The sun set in the West and I sat in the sand while it became cool under my feet and the blackened sky.

I went to the movies alone. Michael Stahlberg gave a gut-wrenching monologue:

"Right now you may not want to feel anything. Perhaps you never wished to feel anything. And perhaps it's not to me that you'll want to speak about these things. But feel something you obviously did…"

I sobbed.

I hadn't made a single new friend in L.A. At the Playhouse. The other students clamored together when we had a break. I stepped outside and stared off into the distance, towards the hills where the celebrities lived. I wasn't giving up on acting, but I was giving up on Hollywood. I thought about meditating again but my body was broken and my mind fractured.

I would have to prevail.

One night Dean invited me to a party in Silver Lake with his acting and modeling friends. Someone had a tattoo gun and despondent hipsters played drinking games. I got a shitty tattoo on the back of my neck, between my shoulder blades. A rising sun, and underneath it, the words "Just Keep Going." It seemed like everyone had a disposable camera at the party, and revelers took pictures that they would post on their blogs. Dean and I took a picture together. He looked like he was full of life, maybe that's what I was really lusting after.

That winter when we were together was the coldest on Boston's record. I had faint memories of hands touching and her blushing when I teased her for kissing another boy that wasn't me. But that was then. Now the air was dry and snow could only be found on a two hour drive up North to Big Bear. Our memories became nights watching pornography filmed in Orange

County and produced in the San Fernando
valley.

*Silver screen fantasies were just that,
fantastical, not real, no more.*

I took Damian's advice and went vegan. I
started drinking again. I didn't care, I was
convinced I never really had a problem.
One night Damian returned from a month at
Sasha's. He returned with the same warmth
he always had.

He asked me how I was doing:

I opened a can of Budweiser and told him
I'd never been better.

I was a liar.

I worked 8 hour days at the construction
site, tearing apart that place a family of four
once called their home. I stuck a cigarette in
my mouth and put a crowbar in my hand,
and pried the rest of my life away every time
the hammer hit the wall. Michel, who had
started doing coke and then stopped at the
precipice where use became an addiction,
called me over to his place off Highland just
below the Hollywood Hills. "You look
terrible," he said. "Yes, I've been drinking

again and I stopped stretching."

"My man," he said, "this is a tough place to be without fame or money."

From his living room windows Hollywood stretched out West, fading into the line where the sun and ocean meet. The sky looked like lavender and I was greeted by the same sign that had welcomed me to this tinsel town and it blinked: "Fame is Fleeting."

5

There seemed to be no plot arc to my time in L.A. Just the persistence of work, and the persistence of the writing — that would begin at dawn and would end when the moon hung over this silver city. The winter months in LA became grayer and dustier by the day. It rained heavily and customers at the coffee house said it hadn't rained like that for years. Work was postponed at the construction site where the grounds had become muddy. The downpours had me thinking of Sedona or somewhere in the Rocky Mountains like Telluride or down off the Florida coast in the keys. Places I'd never imagined before, but were more appealing than ever.

Dean got me a job catering at the Oscars. What next, I thought. Will I become a taxi driver? Garbage man? Postman? In the words of Annie B. (who was funnier than half the women on T.V.) my new job required that I show up and "look like a piece of meat." I'd paint houses or deliver newspapers. I'd work at a carwash. It didn't matter.

My parents wanted me to use my sham of a college degree, but I wasn't interested in sitting behind a desk. I'd rather be out with the men and women that made America work.

My birthday came around Damian's girlfriend Sasha bought me a cupcake. I went to dinner alone. I took a taxi to Santa Monica and watched the sunset on the pier as I contemplated what the hell I was to do next. The Oscars, so what? I didn't care and I wasn't nervous. Celebrity was for me, but only if I could have it.

So, the Oscars came and went: I was lectured by a middle-aged man not to speak to anyone who was rich or famous. I served shrimp cocktails to Danny Glover. I walked past Woody Harrelson. Cameras rolled. Men and women in tuxedos and designer dresses cheered one another, took photos and smiled and laughed. I wore a black suit. I drank a glass of champagne (I wasn't supposed to). One day this could be me. She was going to wear Armani. I was going to wear a tuxedo. I went home and buried my face into my pillow. The party was over. Damian asked me how I was doing. "Not so hot, amigo."

6

I needed to go somewhere, I needed another escape. I thought about returning to Boston, if only briefly. I could stay with my Uncle off the redline, find a studio apartment in Medford, work at a restaurant and write. But Boston was always her town. It didn't matter I had family ties four generations deep.

She adored the city, and the city adored her back. And even when she was gone I couldn't escape her. Once, when we were walking through Boston Common, I told her I'd love her even if she was a boy. We kissed. We held hands. We took a picture together on the bridge that overlooked the pond. We went to a cafe off St. Charles street. I drank coffee, she had espresso. They were playing French music. She translated.

She said it was a song about love and heartbreak. Snow gently fell outside and we huddled in front of the cafe, under an awning, sharing a cigarette, embracing the winter's cold that I had never become accustomed to.

She gave me the world.

I didn't think I had much to offer in return.

One night Damian and I mused over the dining room table some great escape.

"You ever been to Marrakesh?" I asked him.

"No."

"Me Either."

"Why?"

"Heard it's nice."

"Me too."

New years in Marrakesh, that's a laugh. Damian and I couldn't even afford Trader Joe's. We were both young artists looking for our big break. Alas, the only breaks I was getting were smoke breaks on the construction site.

There were billboards all over L.A. advertising on the job injury lawsuits.

I thought about burning myself with scalding hot coffee at the coffee house or driving a nail into my hand.

But I was an honest kid, and somehow took solace in criss-crossing the silver city in a work-driven haze that was both robbing me and giving me my humanity.

The only difference between me and most actors in L.A. was a crowbar and a hammer. I was literally driving myself into the ground digging out trenches for a family of four to have a backyard patio. The foreman said he could get any immigrant in town to the job for half the pay, I considered myself fortunate.

When work was over I would go to the playhouse, and when I went home Damian would be parked in front of the T.V. talking about art direction in Terrence Malik's movies. I could give a damn.

Upstate New York didn't sound too bad either. Tory lived there. She saw me through a drug induced haze in Northern California. She'd take me in. But I couldn't forget about the City. I always thought it was quite possibly the only place I would ever see her again. It was nice to imagine, but on any given day, I had just about enough money to buy two weeks' worth of groceries and a couple packs of cigarettes.

Damian told me to go wherever my heart desired. I picked up another job up at the American Film Center, working as a librarian. I'd take the bus up there to the old repurposed convent in the afternoon, after demolition on the house. The money wasn't good, but it was enough. Each day I came closer to leaving my monastic life in L.A. behind. Damian was stoic as always and I wondered if he was sorry to see me go. Dean was a like a brother but we hardly saw each other outside of work. The nameless actors at the playhouse would forget about me, like I would forget about them.

Bon Voyage L.A.

Buffalo:

Tory lived in Buffalo, so did her sister. She was going to be somebody. She had pink hair and told me that Heaven and Hell had the same gates. She painted with pastels and lived on the Westside with the immigrants and the drug dealers. Buffalo was the closest thing to the border. If the Feds chased me up North, my next stop was Toronto.

I felt like Kerouac.

I wrote like Hemingway.

I was in too deep.

I believed I had been chased out of Los Angeles by the remnants of the Nixon administration. It gave me something to write about. It kept me on the run. It was the only conspiracy theory I ever believed in. The Italians took me in. The polish wanted nothing to do with me. The Irish were nowhere to be found.

Every man in that town told me to get out while I could.

"One pregnancy test and you'll be here for life."

Hannah Hemingway told me guys like me didn't show up to Buffalo often.

Tim recited Ginsberg like it was a mantra over a bottle of wine after work.

Ben Joe, the American Indian, bought me a carton of cigarettes from the Rez.

Karcher published the first 900 words of "The Saints and the Animals."

One Black man with a mouth full of metal told me he was getting a tattoo of the women who had hurt him, and the women who he had hurt.

I ordered another round and I told him I was a Christian.

He asked me what I believed in:

"Mercy and forgiveness."

I blacked out and walked out the door.

Tory texted me that a man with a gold grill didn't make his money in Buffalo selling insurance.

"Crazy world we live in Frank."

"Tell me about it."

I looked her up.

It was time to go.

7

I moved to New York City.

"This is my last fucking shot."

One friend request away from the woman of
my dreams. One drink away from falling
farther into alcoholism. One bag away from
an overdose. None of it mattered.

I loved her.

New York was too much, New York was
not for me. People spilled out of buildings,
pushing and shoving each other. Taxis
congested the streets and honked their horns.
Trains blasted through the tunnels and
subway cars screeched to halt.

Every god damn city I went to wasn't meant
for me, it was meant for her.

Somewhere in the jungle, she was there.

I called all my friends the night I looked her up and she was there. Audrey, Damian, Dean, Michele, and my mother. "Be careful," that's what each person told you. Remember what happened last time you two were together?

"You were so depressed you couldn't work."

"You moved home."

"You never got over her."

"You can't keep going like this."

"Remember in L.A. when you silently went about changing every aspect of your life but still couldn't shake her?"

"Be careful."

We met at the Brooklyn Botanical Gardens. It was late September and summer was giving way to October and the leaves were turning. It was hot but not humid.

I smoked walking in big circles.

I looked a bit mad.

Hell, I had always been a bit mad.

She had seen through that, and I wondered if she could see me out of my alcoholic fog.

She shows up 45 minutes late, and she doesn't apologize. She throws her arms around me and pull me so close to her I can feel her heart beating.

She's hungover and I don't care.

We walked silently for a few minutes, making small talk, looking at the roses, pretending like two years had never passed us by in silence. Pretending that our love died that cold winter. Pretending like we hadn't lost each other one Autumn night when dusk became dawn. Pretending.

It was the best we could do…

8

On a hot summer day in a Bushwick backyard Rosie introduced me to Cuba.

"This nigga looks like Sean Penn."

"I've never heard of Sean Penn."

"You smoke cigarettes when you eat salad?"

"What the fuck are you talking about?"

"You're a goddamn liar."

We shook hands and laughed.

I lit up another cigarette and realized every person at the party looked like a bunch of imposters; rich kids whose parents were paying for them to have some bizarre Brooklyn experience that only someone as possessed as Andy Warhol could dream up.

Cuba thought these rich kids were cute.

Months later I started ripping off my moms to get high with Cuba on coke cut with whatever poison the cartels were pumping out of Mexico. It was an ugly game.

Cuba drank until his speech slurred. I smoked until my lungs burned. We blew coke like it was a prescription drug.

*He had a substance use disorder, I had a
drug abuse problem. We were bound
together by our pain.*

It looked like a suicide pact, but that winter
it would be the only thing that kept me alive.

Cocaine kept us together.

Weeks later we went to a dinner party in
Flatbush, where we drank so much Cuba
passed out on a couch. The conversation
went on past midnight. People wanted to
know what I was doing in New York.

I stammered whenever I spoke.
"Something about writing," I replied.

Mary hosted the party.

She had cheap room in a quiet neighborhood
away from the real estate scheme that was
dismantling Crown Heights.

Most white girls would avoid a place like
this, but she called her neighbors friendly.

She said they were suspicious of her, but
any white kid in a Black neighborhood is
suspicious.

A drug dealer could tell you that.

Mary shrugged it off.

Months earlier I walked two Pitbull's through East New York, dog-sitting for two clueless Christian kids.

I took the dogs out for one stroll, and didn't venture outside again.

There was no reason to cause a commotion.

"Ah hell no."

After dinner, I was shamed for not eating gluten by Joanie's roommate. She said she was "body positive." Weeks prior I thought I was HIV positive.

I guess we had different struggles.

Cuba slept on the couch with his mouth open, snoring. Rosie and I roused him. He stumbled to his feet and lit a cigarette.

"Sean Penn drank me under the table." We called a car and departed into the night…

9

Every night I would climb the fire escape to the roof of my Brooklyn apartment.

Brooklyn itself faded into the downtown skyline, where skyscrapers jetted into the sky like a range of mountains that spread across Manhattan.

She was down there, somewhere. I would stare off into the city, wishing this great big world would bring her and I back together.

When Los Angeles had died out months before Damian and I drank champagne on the balcony. We didn't have much to celebrate, but it still felt congratulatory. "Success is closer than you'd think," Damian said, "It's right around the corner, Frank." We embraced.

 Damian moved to West Hollywood, I moved to New York City.

There were so many places I could have gone. I thought about the no name states with big mountains and winding rivers like Montana, or Wyoming or Utah. Places where it's quiet, I could be with my thoughts. I could have lived in a motel on the outskirts of town. I could have found another drifter. We could have made a life together in the countryside and on the road. I could have gone anywhere, really. But I knew she was there. I couldn't escape her and I didn't want to.

On a cool Autumn night in Times Square after an evening at the playhouse, I thought I glimpsed her in the rush of pedestrians. I went tearing after her, pushing past people, until I became lost in the crowd. I saw her disappear into the New York night, down into the subway, going uptown or off to Brooklyn maybe.

She had glamorous Manhattan and everything I had ever dreamed of but privately resented. It wasn't jealousy, it was heartbreak. I was working two jobs; taking two trains to catch a ride to work; drinking two tall cans of cheap beer every night and smoking one pack of cigarettes each day. I had waited two years to see her again, and now that she was here, I was ashamed to see her.

One night in Boston, we had gone out to the bars with our classmates while I was busy flunking half my classes. We escaped them for a smoke outside. Spring was close to blooming and a cool wind blew into Copley Square from the Bay. She asked me for my jacket, and I wrapped her in it.

We embraced when we both knew we shouldn't have.

One of our classmates asked us if we were in love. We looked each other but we were both afraid to speak. Then she told me she didn't want to hurt me. I told her we were too young to feel pain.

It was September when I took a train out to Coney Island. Cuba and I wandered around the amusement park. The beach was crowded with blankets, umbrellas and people. Kids ran into the ocean escaping the fading heat. I bought a soda and we walked out towards the pier and stood there on the jetty. I was always in contemplation. I was lost in contemplation. I was too busy dreaming. It was much better than facing life...

The summer heat was nauseating. The air was thick and the smog was hard to see through. It was all very tiresome. The tide brought waves into shore. Couples posed for pictures. They held hands and kissed each other on the lips. I made up my mind while I lit a cigarette and stared across the water.

We went out to dinner in October and pretended like we had never had any history. We sat in one of those Indian restaurants in the East Village underneath the swarms of blinking Christmas lights that lit the restaurant. We pretended like we had never discovered one another in the Winter, when the air was warm enough to walk through Jamaica Plain in the dead of night. We pretended like I had never broken down in front of her because she was the first girl I had slept with sober. We pretended that she never told me that she felt shame, too. We pretended like we never got in the fight that drunken night I went looking for her on campus. We pretended we didn't kiss goodbye, when her eyes became wet as she tried not to cry and she told me that it was over. We pretended. That's all we were, we were fucking pretenders.

We became some half-cooked fantasy schemed up by God himself.

We sat down for dinner. She had light dancing in her eyes. She had a body on her. She had an education. She was the only woman I had ever wanted.

We ordered dinner and ate lamb vindaloo
and potato curry. She said it was her
birthday dinner. I picked up the check.

I wanted to tell her the years before we met,
I was in some sort of schizophrenic haze that
I didn't see through until we met. Instead,
she asked about what I was doing in New
York. I forgot about the Feds. I didn't forget
about her.

*"If things don't work out I was gonna move
to Montana and drive a big truck filled with
beets across the State."*

*"I could see you doing that now with your
beard."*

*"What happens when a young person gives
up their dreams?"*

"They get married and have kids."

"Do you want to have kids."

"Yes, I want to name my daughter Alice."

"Alice??"

"Do you want to go for a beer?"

"I went on a road trip, you know?"

"Yeah."

"It just wasn't what I imagined it to be."

"So, what are you doing here?"

"Just writing stories."

"It's just a boyish fantasy."

"I think you're going through a phase."

"I heard a lecture by James Baldwin and it changed my life."

"I'm studying Political Economy at Columbia."

"What happened to Human Rights Law?

"I was young and idealistic."

"That was two years ago."

"I'm leaving in January."

"January."

She was quiet, I was solemn.

It was all we had ever wanted.

I sent her my short story that had been published by a Brooklyn magazine. My one claim to fame.

I had written 50,000 words in a year. 900 of those words were published. She read it on the Subway back to Harlem.

"There was nothing left for us, where the road had ended."

"I like this part," she said, quoting the story.

"Just keep going, no feeling is final." I replied, quoting the same story.

That night, at midnight, she turned 23.

"Happy Birthday, Josie."

10

Madison distracted me afterwards. She took me to a party in Bushwick one night in Winter when trees were bare, left whipped by the wind. "You'll like it," she said, "Maybe you'll meet someone."

I had a crush on Madison.

We met at the cafe I worked at in the East Village. She was cat-like; she had a mind of her own; she could twist her body into a pretzel; she was dating 7 different people and said she broke up with them in a group text.

Her Instagram had 5000 followers. She wore mom jeans and a big black leather jacket. She rolled her own cigarettes. She was wide eyed. She had a pixie cut and jet black hair.

I wanted her like I wanted cocaine.

I needed her like I needed my mother.

I desired a home. She was a resting place.

I wasn't like most of the kids at the party. I wasn't popular like Madison. The partygoers wore second hand designer clothing. They had popular blogs with a few thousand followers. They carried polaroid cameras in their purses and had film cameras slung around their necks. They spent days off venturing into the parts of New York that were seldom seen.

They had explored their sexuality. They had bowl cuts and shaved heads. Their hair was bleach blonde. Their bodies were scattered with tattoos. They had jobs at agencies, magazines, and fashion houses.

They Spirits. They read contemporary poetry and flash fiction. They ran around with socialist and anti-racist organizers. They introduced themselves with their pronouns. They lived in Bushwick and Williamsburg. I figured half of them were bankrolled by their parents, like my coke habit was.

I wasn't boring, but I wasn't like them. I buried myself in my writing, but remained unknown. I was anonymous in the greatest city in the World. I stopped considering what it would feel like to be famous. I asked Madison if she thought I'd make it someday. "Of course you will," she said. "You're the writer." I didn't accept the title. Writing was a grim duty. Frank Bernard was just a part of my imagination.

Like everything else in my life, it wasn't real.

Madison dragged me along to a few photo shoots where she had me hand her clothes while she changed behind a curtain. Each time she walked out and struck different poses and the camera flashed. "This is easy, you could do this," she told me. She laughed, she smiled, she spun around in circles and danced on her tip toes. She was so full of life it should have been contagious.

But there was no changing the grim outlook on life I was reckoning with. Everyone in New York was young and beautiful. They were doing things. They had places to go. I was drinking every night and smoking down a pack of cigarettes by nightfall. It was greener on the other side, but I didn't know how to get there.

Madison took me to Flushing in Queens with her girlfriend Grey. Madison told me that Gray had become suspicious of me. She thought I was trying to make a pass at Madison.

I didn't know what I wanted.

Gray was thin like a rail. She always had a photoshoot. She had been in the magazines. Every week she had a mental breakdown. Madison was trying to rescue her. Some people don't want to be saved.

Madison brought her film camera and took photos of Gray. We walked along the boulevards smoking Madison's e-cigarette. Flushing looked like a Bangkok thoroughfare but still felt like America. The shops were covered in Burmese and Thai and Vietnamese characters. Pedestrians hurried around with their heads to the ground. A rainstorm passed and we ducked into a Japanese restaurant where we were seated and the waiters brought out hot pot. "Frank is heartbroken, Gray, he deserves someone to be kind to him."

I was getting what I deserved.

"What was it like, Asia?" she asked me as we walked through campus on a brisk night. I didn't have much to say while she waived her cigarette around like Brigitte Bardot. I didn't want to tell her I didn't make sense of it until I met her. But it would take me years to piece together a story that would never be published.

Bangkok:

I smoked cheap cigarettes outside of the Burmese embassy in the sweltering tropical heat. My passport was processed and I was told to return in a month. The gates to Myanmar would open but I would have to wait. Each night I would depart into the Bangkok night, venturing further into his depths, seeking out a cure for the loneliness I felt in the West.

There were ceaseless amounts of cheap amphetamines sold on the Bangkok streets. I would get high and go to the bars off Khao San Road, where the Australians and Kiwis would get piss drunk.

Their disdain for the locals; their crassness; how loud they were; their drinking songs; their ignorance. I loathed them.

I knew what I was looking for each night, and the first few weeks in Bangkok I would depart for bed before midnight, knowing the street walkers and lady boys came out when the sun went down.

They would chase me past massage parlors, where girls lined up in fish bowls to do anything you asked them to do if the dollar amount was right. I looked like I was lost when I would pass the women spilling out onto the streets, but I knew what I was looking for, and my innocence could hardly conceal that.

I was staying at a guest house off Sukhumvit in the heart of the city. The guest house was darkly lit, musty and mostly empty, save the rusted ex-pat that owned it and the various Thai women who kept it clean.

I'd spend my days slogging through the Bangkok heat, walking underneath the high rises that shot out from the ground, making it a metropolis. From the sky the city itself appeared like a lucid dream on acid. But it was the underbelly that I kept creeping towards. I would slink around the quiet side streets at night, along the compound walls that lined the road. Neon signs advertising "Girls, Girls, Girls!" would flicker on and off in the distance on the main thoroughfares.

Women would call after me, "Hey honey, come on in." I would retreat to my room, where I drank Tiger beers alone, and took to touching myself in the shower. I didn't want to give in but the darker side of Bangkok begged me to join it, and so I did.

The University wanted me to spend my research grant on my undergraduate thesis in bullshit.

I had other ideas.

The brothel was away from the flashing lights of the redlight districts. It was hidden among the compound walls, away from the prying eyes of the foreigners I disdained. My heart raced and I felt like each stranger I passed knew where I was going and what I was doing. I hadn't a drink in me but I had taken some amphetamine. I slipped through the entryway and was met by an older Thai woman with spectacles who sat behind a desk.

The woman led me through a set of swinging doors, and there, behind a transparent glass bubble, were 20 or so women wearing underwear and lingerie.

They looked like they had been picked out of a catalogue for swimwear. My eyes met an older woman's behind a glass fishbowl where the women collected.

She appeared weathered in a beautiful way, and each time I scanned the women behind the glass bowl, my eyes returned to hers.

There had been a virgin-like disposition when our eyes met. I motioned to see her and she walked out from behind the glass and took my hand and led me up to a private room.

"I've never done this before," I told her. "If this is your first time, it's OK." She said, in an accent that wasn't practiced but was heavy.

She carefully stripped me of my undergarments, undoing my belt and unbuttoning my jeans. She caressed and massaged me until I was weakened in the knees and hard. She was gentle but I released quickly and laid there, unable to speak, my face numb in the afterglow of orgasm. She kissed me on the mouth. I limped back into the rush of Bangkok, the sky glowing as evening turned to night.

12

Cash loved Dylan.

He looked like James Dean.

He talked like Brando.

The world saw Cash.

I saw Alan.

Cuba and I looked out for him while
Madison kept me alive.

We met at the playhouse in midtown, where
he would sit alone in the top row of the seats
above the stage, smoking an e-cigarette,
brooding. I continued to pretend I was an
actor. It gave me an identity. It gave me
something to do. This wasn't Los Angeles.

If I couldn't be in Hollywood, I could be on
Broadway. Cash was an actor. I was an
imposter.

One night after class he confronted me:

"Are you really in this thing?"

"Yeah."

"Yeah, but are you in it for life?"

"I never really thought about it — "

"I'm in it for life, man. I don't care how
long it takes. That's how you have to be,
man. You have to become obsessed with it.
It has to become your obsession. You gotta
wake up every morning thinking about these
characters, man. When you get in the
shower, you're saying your lines. When

you're on the subway you're reading a play. When you're an actor you act. It's pure, unadulterated obsession, man. But uh, don't take my word for it, read about the greats. Brando, Pacino, all these guys, they made this their lifeblood. Look at me man, do you believe me?"

"Yeah," I laughed, "I believe you! I really do."

"So, I'm gonna ask you again, are you in this? Like, really in this?"

"Yeah, I'm *fucking* in this."

Fame was always my only answer to the hardships and the depression that had rattled me in my college years. But mostly, I thought it would be my only way back to her. It was a hopeless cause.

The playhouse was on 45th in midtown crammed between jewelry shops and take out spots. Across the street was a dive bar where business men would unwind from their days making our economy work. There wasn't an actor in the class besides Cash who had a future on the silver screen. But we would gather in the bar, and discuss the futures none of us had.

I had always dreamt of being on the Tonight Show. I told Cash that if we ever became famous I would ride a horse on to the set of the Tonight Show.

"Well, Jimmy, I was down at the border drinking tequila with my buddy Don Pablo." Cash called me "one crazy motherfucker."

I lost my mind.

13

I lived in a hole of an apartment in Brooklyn with an African named James. It was close enough to Atlantic that you could hear the cars speed through the black of night. Clothes were scattered across the floors of my room and dishes piled up in the sink. The apartment was empty. There was only a couch, a coffee table and an unused bench press.

Cuba called it a trap house.

I smoked out of the window, and discarded cigarettes lay in an ashtray on the window sill. There was no art on the walls save a picture of Malcolm X. Books piled up on the ground where there should have been shelves. It was the type of the place that you wouldn't want to hang around in.

This was the only place I could afford a room of my own.

I didn't know my neighbors. But I knew D'Angelo. D'Angelo lived down the hall from my apartment with his family. He was buddies with James. We met on the roof one night while he rolled a blunt with James and I had a smoke.

"What's good bro?"

We became acquainted and he came around to smoke in my apartment when hands would become numb in the winter cold. D'Angelo would play raggaetone, roll out his fronto and get stoned.

We would have beers and watch sports on T.V. Sometimes D'Angelo would come over with his boys from the neighborhood, play French Montana, and we would get rightfully drunk and stoned.

They would call me "Peter Parker," and let me hit the blunt.

D'Angelo had a baby girl. I asked D'Angelo

about his girlfriend.

"That's my baby's mother bro," he said.

"She's my queen."

Everyone had someone.

I'd become placid when I got high with D'Angelo. I'd fall asleep on the couch. D'Angelo asked me why I looked so down. I told him it was something about depression. "Aye, my moms got that too," he said. "You should try exercising, I read somewhere that helps."

There was always something going on. James knew half of Brooklyn and they would make music and play dancehall until the sun came up. I'd come home after work and there would be girls drinking cognac and dancing in the living room.

James would greet me with a big smile, and shout "Pull up!" I holed up in my room instead, listening to dharma talks that were somehow gonna get me through all of this.

Sometimes I would sneak out for some cognac and talk to James' cousin Kristopher who ran a Hotel up in the Bronx. I was always the odd one out, a white kid from Southeast Portland. They were Black but they embraced me as one of their own.

It was home.

Each morning I rose at dawn to work, blindly throwing on clothes and cramming a play into my coat pocket. I would limp to the bodega on the corner and get a tall black coffee. The train was across Atlantic avenue and I would dodge cars zooming down the speedway. I'd light a cigarette and smoke it until I reached the station. When Winter hit, I wore wear two pairs of wool socks, a flannel, a sweater and my overcoat. I stuffed my hands into my pockets, and braced myself against the cold.

The train was filled with the working people of New York. As the train rattled through Brooklyn, passengers would be asleep in their seats, nodding awake every time the train jostled around. They were construction workers, they were fast food workers, they worked in anonymity and weren't celebrated. They were the ones that made this world work. They didn't have 401K's, they were uninsured, they were living paycheck to paycheck, they had a few jobs and families to feed. They went to work, and didn't ask for mercy.

This town opened its doors to the well-to-do and well-connected. Cash introduced me to people as a writer. I didn't accept the title. Writing was a grim duty, Frank Bernard was fantastic, so was my life, so were my dreams. Living in my head was much better than starving myself to get high on the weekends.

Meanwhile, Cuba and I watched a generation of young men who loved their mothers be crucified on the internet by white women with liberal arts educations. They were the art dealers, they were the curators, they were the literary agents. They were on T.V. and on editorial boards. They wanted to be victims. I could give a damn.

The artists, the writers, the unknowns, they were left to fight their way out of the bottom. Their pain was their work. Their humility was their downfall. Our only chance at a shot at this shit was to be discovered by the pretentious graduates of New England liberal arts schools.

The artists, the writers, the unknowns, they would create their works in the throes of America, in the neighborhoods touched by poverty and crime. Their work would be discovered decades later, and the places they once called home would be priced out by the wealthy who lived in outsized condominiums. The wealthy would display their works on coffee tables and on their walls. They were pushed closer and closer to the edge. I wasn't sure if it was worth it, but I kept writing.

14

I invited Josie to a holiday party in Chinatown to celebrate Thanksgiving. She asked if she could bring a friend. I told Jerry I was bringing a VIP. She told me she was bringing a boy. She said they were "just friends." I got angry and asked her if we were "just friends." She said yes, because I'm still with Jacque, or Felix, or Loris or whatever the fuck his French name was.

Why was she ever gonna show up in the first place? So we could pretend we never happened?

I went to a liquor store in Chinatown and bought a bottle of wine. I smoked a pack down before she got to the party. I told Jerry that every girl from the Upper West Side sounded the same in bed.

"It must be a liberal arts school thing."

He almost died laughing.

She arrived with a French girl who told me she was going to teach me how to French kiss. I drank another glass of wine and contemplated planting one on her friend.

I was in a sour mood.

I told Josie men were like dogs.

She told me she preferred cats.

I poured another glass of Port.

We had Thanksgiving dinner. Jerry asked what was wrong. Josie stared me down from across the table. I stared back.

I poured her another glass of red.

She told me she had felt guilt.

She was the only thing holding me together as America descended into madness.

We went out for a cigarette. She asked why everyone at the party was Jewish. I shrugged and said something about multi-culturalism in the Trump era.

I told her I'd tweet about it.

She wanted to leave:

I grabbed her by the wrist.

She slapped me away.

I doubled down on my grip.

She tried to call a car.

I went for her phone.

She ripped me apart.

I grabbed her by the arm.

She pushed me away.

I kissed her friend on the cheek.

"Take care of her."

It was over.

15

"Listen buddy, you're not getting her back," Cuba told me at a dive in Brooklyn. It was Sunday night. I called my dealer and Cuba paid for the bag. I bought another round. We weren't playing around.

I told him there were days in L.A. when I would talk out loud like she was still around, speaking to someone I hardly knew about this dream that could not be replaced. I told him there was New York, when she was one train away, but had never felt so far away. I told him about Thanksgiving.

"You're not supposed to get her back,"
Cuba said, "She's gone."

Winter would come and go like she had. But it was still March and the thought of warmer weather was like a dream you could not remember.

That night I met a girl. I told her I studied "Media, Culture and Society," in college. Then I went on a rant about Jesus Christ. She told me I was the most handsome boy at the bar. I asked her if she liked coke, "I love it," she replied. We blew through a bag in the bathroom.

We went home together and she talked until the sunshine bled through the windows of my bedroom. She asked me what my greatest fear was (it was never seeing Josie again). I was too weak to speak. I didn't answer her. Then she asked me if I was dominant. I told her I could be whatever she wanted. We slept for three hours. She asked me why I looked so sad. "I just don't know anymore." She asked me if we'd see each other again. I told her we were like "two ships passing in the night." She gave me head before she left. It was all downhill from there:

I had two one night stands. Both of the girls were from Florida. I claimed I was bisexual. Cocaine was always part of the picture. We got high and took off all our clothes. They were beautiful. But when we finished, I would gather my clothes and take off into the New York night, looking for more ways to remedy my brokenness.

I started seeing a therapist that specialized in love-addiction. The only thing we talked about were my star-signs and sex-life. He told me to sober up. I told him I was going on an internet date.

She showed up with neon blue hair and a tight black dress. I showed up armed to the teeth:

A pint of whiskey, a pack of Marlboros and my dealer's # on speed dial.

We left the party early. She wanted a bag and she paid for it. We painted to PARTYNEXTDOOR. She took out her point and shoot camera. I was naked, holding onto a pillow like a new born child. Months later she sent the picture to me. I looked like John F. Kennedy Jr. strung out on cocaine. It was never my intention. That night I did blow until dawn cast a pink light over downtown Manhattan. She slept like a baby and kissed me goodbye.

Cuba called me at 4 A.M.

"I'm cooking breakfast."

I called a car and we drank Tecate over toast.

We took a picture on the roof.

"My dawg."

D'Angelo told me not to fuck with that shit

anymore. Cuba and I didn't heed his advice.

Weeks later the girl with neon blue hair texted me:

"Are you into guy on guy?"

"I'm curious."

She wanted a dude to blow me while she watched.

I said no.

"I knew you weren't gay."

I was confused.

Cuba and I went from bar to bar while I looked for more women who could remove me from my misery. Most boys would brag. I told Cuba I didn't know what was wrong with me. Cuba told me there were plenty of fish in the sea. Then he told me Carmelo Anthony was the G.O.A.T.

My sexless and sober days in L.A. seemed far away, but I didn't want them back. It was then that I even recalled the meditation hall, and more so recalled the boy who had not yet found out the truth about love but had found solace in religion.

"What did that ever do for me?" I asked out loud one night as I paced around thinking of ways to beat back addiction.

Nothing at all.

I got another job at a sushi restaurant. I worked 19 days in a row without a day off. I ate one dollar pizza. I went to Yoga and sat in corpse pose for 45 minutes. I met a literary agent. They went in a "different direction." Cash and I went to a Columbia bar and I told a group of girls I studied linguistics at MIT. Cash took the prettiest one home. I was alone at the bar and drank myself into a hole. I fell in love with the bartender at 1020. She bought me a bag of blow and I blew her a kiss. Then I sent a girl I met on Tinder naked pix. I threw up in the Uber on the way home.

I started a party that I couldn't leave.

My buddy Bryan told me about recovery.

"10 states in 10 years, you can't run forever kid."

I didn't listen.

I stopped taking medication because it fucked with my highs and bought viagra on the internet. *Shit got dark.* D'Angelo stopped coming around. Cuba told me we were in too deep. I did coke alone, I did coke with friends, I did coke before work and after work. I spent the next three months drunk, high, coming down or hungover. I had started a party that I couldn't leave. Cuba said I wasn't getting her back. I was too fucked up to cry.

C'est La Vie.

16

I quit writing. I wanted to quit the playhouse, but Cash wouldn't let me. He told me we were in this together. I had sent short stories to several magazines but there was no fanfare or calls from agents heralding me as the next great American voice. I had missed my shot by a decade. What could a white kid like me contribute to the national discourse?

One romance. A few addictions but drug memoirs were out of date. I had mental conditions, but so did everybody. I had been in love once, maybe twice, but who fucking cares right? I had traveled, but what had I ever learned? If I didn't learn how to love myself now, could I ever? Who was I to deserve a happy ending? Who was I to ever have dreamed? I was just another white man in America. I was owed nothing, but had once believed I would have everything. My heroes would be judged by history to be deeply flawed men. History would judge me to be the same.

17

"I love feeding Frankie." Benji said while he rifled through his refrigerator, looking for the leftovers from last night. I was on my last legs, and Benji could see it. There were bags under my eyes. I didn't wear socks. I slept in my jeans. I showed Benji Madison's blog. "This girl actually talks to you?" He said. "It's just platonic." I responded. Benji gave me a back rub, "Baby, you're money."

"C'mon bro, she's not that special," Benji told me when I told him of my sadness. I told him he was wrong. "OK, so what, maybe this was the wrong place, wrong time," he replied. I took a beer out of Benji's fridge and downed it. I couldn't drink myself out of this. But I would try. "You should call my cousin Max. He's got the best hands in Manhattan. What you need is a massage."

Madison recounted her father's drug days. She told me how he got away. He moved overseas and never looked back. Cuba told me he couldn't keep going. I believed there was no saving me. Not even Jesus could do it. I went to mass at Saint Patrick's cathedral. I stood near the alter and cried.

Everyone had some advice. Everyone had a story to tell. Everybody thought they knew the answer. Madison got real with me. "Frank, you need help." I wanted to be rescued, cry on her shoulder, a kiss on the lips. She held my hand. She checked on me. She took me to A.A. They said "liquor was just the symptom."

Madison took me to a doctor.
They drugged me up.

"You know what your problem is?" Cuba said to me on his stoop one evening. "You fall too hard. You see a girl and imagine your whole life with her. You're mad when it comes to love. Rosie thinks you're sex crazed. I know the truth. It's the same reason you get high. You get to runaway. You get away from Frank Bernard. Love is your escape." He continued: "I love you, so does

Rosie, but someone needs to tell you these things." I thought about phoning someone. Madison maybe. But I knew better, we weren't like that. There were millions of people living in this terrible town and I had no one to call. I was alone.

18

Waking up was impossible. Putting on clothes was hard. Walking to the subway was harder. Drinking at night was a reward. I bought tall cans of beer from the bodega. D'Angelo would knock on the door every night. He would come over and get high and I would get drunk. This happened three, maybe four times a week.

Some nights I was too tired to answer the door. Forgive me, D'Angelo.

Every once in a while D'Angelo would bring his girl and their kid around. We turned on cartoons and we would sit around the couch, his daughter resting in his arms. We were both in our 20s, but D'Angelo was already a man. He had a family, he had tiresome work, he carried himself differently. I had no responsibilities to anyone other than myself.

It all felt selfish, I didn't know any other way.

I wanted the world for D'Angelo and his girl and their daughter. I wanted it more than I wanted it for myself. I wanted the unfairness of this world to pass them by, lay claim to someone else, someone not as good and not as gracious…

Winter continued into March. It made me numb. The cold rendered me lifeless. The skies were always gray. Sometimes the sun poked through the clouds. The light wasn't bright. It was faint and yellow. Spring was somewhere in the distance. It seemed like a long ways down the road. Cash would call me up to go to the bars with the Columbia girls. He told me they were convinced I was some sort of linguistics whiz who had graduated MIT magma cum laude. I told him I couldn't because I could barely dress myself in the morning.

There was always some lousy excuse.

Sometimes I envied Cash, sometimes I was afraid for him. He had his youth, he had his anger and he had his passion. He would pull me aside at the Playhouse, and demand to know how I felt about the world. I told him I hoped our fate was in the hands of a merciful God. Then he told me about being alone:

"Solitude man, Rilke wrote about it in Letters to a Young Poet. You know Rilke? When I first got here, I was alone, and I wandered the city by myself. I wasn't supposed to be living here, man. New York was gonna eat me alive and you know how I beat it back? I embraced loneliness. Solitude is what every man has sought at the crossroads of their lives. That's your answer."

"I believe you." I told him. (Like I didn't know a damn thing about the world.)

The Playhouse was crammed into midtown and shared the same block as the Harvard Club. We would walk past it every night longing for success. From the street, you could see inside. It was dressed with chandeliers and velvet curtains. Wait staff were dolled up to serve patrons whose wealth we could not comprehend. On a cold night in March Cash jumped up next to the windows and pounded on the glass until it cracked. Cash was losing it in the cold and the poverty of it all. He beat his chest like a gorilla. Patrons looked on with fear. He made faces at these rich folks. He looked like a caged animal. We got chased away by the doormen and went running down the street.

Nights later we went out for beers after rehearsal at the playhouse. Cash drank heavily. He was silent and smoked his e-cigarette blowing the smoke in every direction. He was lost in his own mind. We went to McDonald's.

Vagrants hung around McDonald's. It was a few blocks of Times Square. One of the vagrants knocked into Cash. Cash took exception to it and he violently swung at the man. The blow caught the man on the cheek. He swung back. The two started brawling. I tried to drag Cash out of the McDonald's but he still wasn't finished. He lunged at the man and got on top of him. He swung and he swung. Blood was everywhere. I grabbed Cash and tried to pull him away. Cash swung at the man and caught me on the chin. I blacked out. Someone called the cops. I went running into the subway. Cash followed.

"What the fuck is the matter with you man?!" I demanded. "I don't know," replied Cash. Then he started sobbing. I grabbed

Cash and hugged him. His train arrived and he went into the night.

I was rattled.

I deleted my dealer's phone number and called Cash a few days later. He didn't pick up so I went to his restaurant on Park avenue to track him down. He was there, and upon seeing me he told me he was a peacemaker now. I told him he could've gotten hurt. He shrugged and told me he had picked up Ginsberg and was dedicating himself to poetry.

Cash told me he had been doing something thinking about me too and suggested I should move to New Jersey. "You can get a cheap apartment on the other side of the river and just write. No distractions, just the writing. You can come into the city whenever you want to, just to walk around and get inspiration." This didn't sound like a bad idea, but I told him I would spend the next few weeks in contemplation about what came next.

When Kerouac got off the road he drank himself to death. I had different plans. What about Denver or Detroit? What about Colorado or Arizona? What about tall mountains and wide open spaces? What about big skies and starry nights? What about the Carolina coasts or the Florida Keys? What about New York City?

I knew something about the world; that once you set foot in the world, you belonged to it and it belongs to you and it will be lonely and poetic and nothing else. Not many people see the poetry in the world, the sad poetry of it all. The ones who do, they are the unlucky ones, they are the lonesome few.

Yangon:

My cheeks stained red, my jawline soft, my body tall and thin, my face bare. I had spent too much money in Thailand so I figured I would stick around Yangon as long as I could. I stayed in a hostel downtown in a windowless room where the air conditioner could barely keep up with the heat seeping through the cracked walls.

Outside the walls, tenement buildings were crammed together, almost falling on top of each other. Old colonial buildings in terrible disrepair were found every few blocks, people spilling out from under them. Taxis filled the streets, honking their horns them in the afternoon traffic. Vendors filled the streets. They sold portraits of the democratic leader and ripped off Hollywood movies made in China and distributed across Asia. Men chewed something like a coca leaf and spat red stained saliva onto the sidewalks.

The sun bled through a tropical rainstorm and pedestrians huddled under umbrellas. Men wore long skirts that covered the ankles and white dress shirts stained by the smog and sweat. The rain cleared the air of the smell of gasoline and cigarette smoke. Monks walked in line in orange robes carrying their alms bowls. Women would retreat out of their stalls and feed them. In the hills there was wealth to be found, foreign dignitaries and men in international business in gated townships. But not here. People would stare at me in the streets, vendors would beckon me into their stalls, dogs ran around untethered, taxi drivers would waive me inside their cars.

"American!"

I was lost but I wasn't scared.

She always asked what happened in Myanmar. I told her that there wasn't much to tell but when she asked, I wanted to tell her the truth.

I wanted to tell her about Pearl and how we criss-crossed Myanmar on an express bus to the mountains and back; how we listened to Pho Aung read poetry; how she wrapped her arms around me on the back of a motorbike in Shan State; and how we fought off feelings we had for each other because it was our only way out. I thought about Sue; driving around in a Porsche with her friends in the dead of the Yangon night; drinking whiskey, going from bar to club to VIP section; kickboxing in the townships, sparring with Lone Chaw in the tropical heat; teaching Orwell in the ghettos on the outskirts of town; the Russian teacher; the kareoke joint in Maymyo; racing through a monsoon with a military man slumped over my back…

Holding on for dear life..

Our last night on Myanmar's coast Pearl told me I didn't belong. We stayed in an empty hotel that sat on the ocean. Tom drank me under the table playing cards. I lost every hand and he kept pouring whiskey while he questioned every motive a foreigner would have in a country where exports meant money and money meant crime.

He took me to the house.

I was never much for gambling. It was a liar's game. I did what I always did. Lose a good hand, and throw my chips on the table. I emptied my pockets.

We ended up in an empty club where a DJ played hypnotic techno and Russian foreigners who looked like me stared in our direction. Pearl's apathy became despair. My despair became loathing. We drank until we couldn't speak and we could hardly walk as we stumbled out of the club and we fell down near the Gazebo.

"Do you want to go to the beach?" I said feebly, broken beyond recall, as pitch black night spun all around me.

"Just take me home."
"Ok."

I picked her slight frame up, and stumbled to her hotel room where I dropped her on the bed before I blacked out in my room and Tom snored. Empty bottles, money and cigarette butts lay strung across the balcony floor.

The next morning I waded into the water, head pounding, bobbing in the salt water thinking about how small this world was, believing fate hadn't brought me here, but bad luck had. The West wasn't for me, but the East had brought me to my knees. I got out of the water and spied Pearl hovering near the buffet that looked over the ocean, gazing out beyond the horizon.

"Where are you going? Your bags are packed?" She asked me.

I looked away.

"You're a good guy, you know that?"

"Yeah." I said, sheepishly.

We embraced.

19

Josie sent me on a journey, I wasn't lost but I was scared. But I wasn't the only one. Cash was on the journey too, and always had a fatal look in his eyes, like this dream was the only thing keeping him alive. Cuba was as well, every time he drank until dawn and jumped on the subway to work himself to the bone. Madison had made it to the other side, but I didn't know what that looked like or felt like. Maybe I had been there, in a past life.

Josie, man. It was the night we disappeared into Boston that did me in. That night my ghosts didn't follow us as we walked through Jamaica Plain. That night she held onto my arm like my mom would when she was proud of me. That night I was too young to foresee how this journey would push us apart. That night I didn't know I would walk it alone. That night I remembered all of her words. That night time stood still, and we stood together. That night James Baldwin's words ran through my head and out of my mouth. That night I promised myself something I couldn't tell her. That night I was 23.

There was who I had been, and there was who I was going to become. And she had been a witness. That night we didn't talk about red carpets or flashing cameras, we spoke about what was required of us. That night we spoke about silence and its consequences. That night we spoke about the poets. Only the poets know the truth about us: Statesmen don't, priests don't, soldiers don't, only the poets. That night never belonged to us. That night there was longing but that night we were the honest to God truth. We spoke quietly, and kissed in the Boston streets. We walked slowly and shared cigarettes. We held onto each other when it was time to say goodbye. And we were holding onto something that I would never let go.

There had been too many days when I would run the events of that night through my head, trying to recapture what we had shared. The nights when I was in the mountains, putting my head back together, when I would rewrite that night over and over again. There were days in L.A. when I would talk out loud like she was still around, speaking to someone I hardly knew about this dream that could not be replaced. There was New York, when she was one train away, but had never been farther from the night we disappeared. There was the night Cuba told me I would never get her back.

Maybe I wasn't supposed to.

My dreams were waning, my visions of stardom had decreased. But I had written hundreds of pages. The times I sent my writing out, I had been met with rejection letters and politely worded emails. My voice couldn't stand on its own. I wrote the

hardscrabble of life: the tiredness on the
subway cars at dawn; days aimlessly
wandering around the village; in the nights
drinking alone…

*I had found meaning in a life that was meant
for her.*

20

June arrived and with it the summer heat.
Air conditioners hummed. Pedestrians
walked on the shaded parts of the street.
People barbequed in their yards and drank
lemonades. Children played in the street.
Cuba, Cash and Madison came over one
night. They were all leaving. Madison to a
photoshoot in Paris. Cash had a role in a
film down in California. Cuba was going on
tour. I would stay but I so desperately
wanted to leave.

We gathered on the roof and drank ice tea
and smoked cigarettes. A great storm rolled
off the Atlantic and a mighty wind blew
across New York. Thunder clapped in the
distance and lightning struck downtown. We
retreated inside. I opened the windows in my
apartment as rain poured from the skies.
Madison stood at the window and watched
New York darken. Cash sprawled out on my
bed reading a play. Cuba sat on the couch

and hummed a solemn tune. I listened to the
rain dance across the pavement and strike
the windows. In the distance, somewhere on
the horizon, the sun swung down like a great
pendulum. The storm passed. Everything
was quiet.

Epilogue

I meditated for 3 days and 3 nights. In the
meditation hall the laymen nodded awake
each morning at 5 A.M. while the monks
roused me when I slept under my mosquito
net and on my cushion.

On my way out the door an old Chinese man
from Chicago wandered down the road away
from the gates of the meditation hall while I
walked towards them. He broke his silence.

"You are going to live a very long life," he
told me, before he walked down the road.

I stood there, lit a cigarette and kept going.

John Francis is a young writer looking to take off. He was born in Portland, OR. He was previously published in the July 2018 issue of the New York based Ghost City Review.

IG: @lonesomeones
COVER ART: @alecvanstav

Made in the USA
Las Vegas, NV
31 March 2021